First published in 2006 by
Franklin Watts
338 Euston Road
London
NW1 3BH

Franklin Watts Australia
Hachette Children's Books
Level 17/207 Kent Street
Sydney
NSW 2000

A CIP catalogue record for this book is available
from the British Library.

ISBN 0 7496 6591 2 (hbk)
ISBN 0 7496 6808 3 (pbk)

Series Editor: Jackie Hamley
Series Advisor: Dr Barrie Wade
Series Designer: Peter Scoulding

Printed in China

Captain
Cool

by Damian Harvey

Illustrated by Rory Walker

FRANKLIN WATTS
LONDON•SYDNEY

If you're stuck in a jam
or a tight fix,

who will be there
in just two ticks?

"Captain Cool!" we shout.
"That's who!

"You should see what
he can do!"

His rocket shoes can outrun a train.

His power suit takes him higher than a plane.

His infra-red eyes
can see in the dark.

And with bulging arms,
he swims like a shark.

Monsters and villains had
best watch out,

if Captain Cool is

hanging about.

When Wild West Jack
rode into town,
to steal the mayor's
golden crown ...

Captain Cool soon
foiled his plans,

and squashed his
robots like tin cans.

When four-eyed monsters
came from Mars,
and started eating
people's cars ...

21

Captain Cool just shouted: "STOP!"

Then sent them home
with a "BIFF! POW! BOP!"

Monsters don't bother
Captain Cool –

not even a gigantic ghoul.

But there is one thing
that makes him shake,